THE STORIES OF VANISHING PEOPLES

The stories
of vanishing peoples

A book for children prepared by
John Mercer
Illustrated by Tony Evora

Allison & Busby
London • New York

To David

First published 1982 by
Allison and Busby Limited
6a Noel Street, London W1V 3RB
and distributed in the USA by
Schocken Books Inc
200 Madison Avenue, New York, N.Y 10016

British Library Cataloguing in Publication Data

Mercer, John
  Stories of vanishing peoples.
  1. Mythology − Juvenile literature   2. Children's
  literature
  I. Title
  398.2'024054   PZ8.1

  ISBN 0-85031-421-6
  ISBN 0-85031-422-4 Pbk

Set in 12/14pt Imprint by Alan Sutton Publishers
and printed in Great Britain by
The Camelot Press, Southampton.

Contents

About these vanishing peoples and their stories

The peoples whose stories make up this book have had different histories and will probably have different futures. Some, like the original inhabitants of Brazil, seem likely to die out altogether – following the Ona people of the very south of South America, the last of whom died a few years ago. Others, such as the Eskimos and the Bushmen, will lose their old ways of life and come to live much like the rest of the world. Most of them will have miserable lives compared to their old ways, for they are not prepared for the sort of life that the rest of the world lives.

Why does this happen? It has been going on for six hundred years, since the Europeans began to spread around the world. They have been steadily taking away the lands of the native peoples. They did this first so that they could put animals to graze on them and could grow crops on them. They also wanted to cut down and take away the trees and to collect up valued products such as gold, rubber, dyes and so on. Now, in the 1980s, the lands of the native peoples are wanted for their oil, uranium and other minerals used by our technically more-advanced peoples.

Because of all this, the native peoples have not been able to go on living in their old ways: they had no forests in which to hunt, no land for their own animals and crops. And, until about a hundred years ago, many of them were being caught and made into slaves by the invading peoples. Many still have to work for them, doing the worst jobs for very little pay: they know no other way to make their livings.

But many of those who have resisted the Europeans over the hundreds of years were killed. The last of these battles are still being fought, for example in Brazil.

Many of the vanishing peoples are nomads – they move around huge areas, usually deserts, hunting and driving herds of animals. Because nomads are hard to control, many governments try to make them settle down in one place, live in houses and take up paid work. So, though many will survive as people, their old way of life is soon forgotten.

So it will not be long before these peoples or at least their ways of life have vanished. Does it matter? Many people think it does. There are two main reasons.

First, because all human beings have a right to live their own lives just as they wish, so long as they do not disturb other people. Those who have invaded the native peoples did not have to do so: it is simply that they have been and still are greedy for more land, animals and money.

The second reason is that the world will lose much by the vanishing of these peoples and their very special ways of living. Not only are they interesting but the native peoples know many things that the rest of us have forgotten or have never known. And the more of them who disappear, the more the world will look the same from end to end.

Their stories are very special too. Most of the peoples who feature in this book have never needed to read or write. Whenever they had something to tell each other, they did so by simply speaking; there was always plenty of time because life was often easy and calm. There was much story-telling: it brought people together more than, say, reading a book by oneself.

The older people often told stories to the younger ones, so that the stories were also their own people's history. They also held their beliefs: how the world was made, how the animals came to be the way they are, where good ideas have come from and why people behave the way they do. Many native peoples believe they are descended from animals of different kinds: that's why, in some stories, men and women change easily into animals and animals often act like human beings. However, to really understand every part of their stories it would be necessary to have lived like the story-tellers, for they know and feel much more than we do about the plants and animals around them.

The stories also show how two or more peoples, though they live in different parts of the world, can have the same stories — it isn't always easy to explain this. For example, there are many stories about a great flood. The stories also show how native peoples are all concerned about the same things, like the sun and how man first got fire. And these stories are also told by our own peoples – those of the readers of this book – underlining how our ancestors shared the past with the forefathers of the native peoples.

Soon there will be little but their stories left of these vanishing peoples. To let them disappear rather than help them to survive will be to take part in one of the world's saddest stories.

Jaboti plays his flute

(Tupis of the Brazilian jungle)

One day, somewhere in the middle of the forests and
the swamps, Jaboti the tortoise was sitting outside his
hole and playing the flute. He did not hear a man
creeping up on him – and, suddenly, he was caught!

The man put Jaboti in a basket and carried him
back to his hut. Then he went off to hunt for more
food. His two children were pounding up roots by the
door of the hut.

After a while the girl said: "I can hear beautiful
music."

"It seems to be coming from the basket!" exclaimed
the boy. He opened the lid. "It's a tortoise," he said,
in surprise. "He's playing the flute."

Jaboti now spoke: "I can dance even better."

"Let's put him on the floor," said the girl. She
lifted the tortoise out of the basket.

Jaboti, standing on his back legs, danced back-
wards and forwards and round and round, with little
hops and jumps now and then. Then he stopped and
said: "You won't mind if I go out for a pee, I'll only
be a moment."

When, after a long time, Jaboti had not come back, the boy and girl became afraid. "Father will be very cross that we've let that tortoise get away," said the boy.

The girl ran out and came back with a flat stone with a round back. "Quick!" she cried. "You make us some paint."

It was almost dark when their father came back. He went at once towards the basket. "Let's have the tortoise for supper."

The boy said: "It's already in the pot."

The man peered inside and saw what looked like the shell of a tortoise. He nodded. Then he poured some water into the pot and put it over the fire.

After the water had boiled for a while, the man said: "Supper's ready." He picked up the pot and emptied it out over a big flat dish.

The heavy stone rolled out and broke the dish. "Oh – it's been turned to stone, I must've cooked it too long!" cried the man.

But at the same moment they all heard the sound of a flute being played a long way away. Jaboti was home again.

Why people are different

(Tupis of the Brazilian jungle)

Sacaibou, the father of all men, was walking across a plain. "Why, a piece of cloud must have fallen from the sky!" he exclaimed. Something white covered the branches of one of the trees. But, when he reached it, Sacaibou saw it was a cotton tree. "Hmm, this looks useful," he said aloud. "I'll take some seeds home."

Sacaibou planted them by the river. Soon they turned into little trees and were growing well. Sacaibou went off on a hunting trip. But when he got back he found the trees had been torn up. He planted some more but, each time he left them, the growing trees were torn up again. As there was nobody else on the earth then but his son Rairou, Sacaibou knew that it must be his work.

So he decided to punish Rairou. He found a *tatu* – that's the Tupis' name for the armadillo – and put some glue on his tail. "Please go into your hole but leave your tail sticking out," Sacaibou said to him.

The *tatu* did so. Soon Rairou came by. He grabbed the tail of the *tatu*, meaning to eat him, and tried hard to pull him out. But Sacaibou had chosen the strongest of the *tatus* and, instead, it was Rairou who

was dragged down into the hole. He could not let go of the sticky tail and was taken deep into the earth.

At last he managed to get free. Lost, he wandered through many tunnels. He met all sorts of men and women and animals. In the end he found himself among a kind and handsome people. And they showed him the way home.

While he had been out of the way, Sacaibou's trees had been able to grow and bear fruit – in fact Sacaibou was now spinning the cotton bolls into the first thread. Rairou told him about his journey. But all the time he was thinking out a way to be revenged on his father.

Rairou asked: "Why don't you bring up some of those beautiful people to live on the earth?"

"All right," agreed Sacaibou.

So Rairou went down again into the hole of the *tatu*. Sacaibou sat at the top, letting down a long strong thread of his new cotton. After a while he felt something light on the end. He quickly pulled up a man and a woman. Looking at them closely as he untied them from the thread, Sacaibou saw great kindness and beauty in their faces. He smiled as he watched them go off. "They're just what we need," he thought.

He dropped the line down again. Feeling a new and heavier pull, Sacaibou excitedly hauled away . . . on the end this time were four ordinary-looking men and women. He shrugged his shoulders as he watched them making their way off round the world.

For the third time Sacaibou let down his thread. This time it took him a good deal of pulling to get the bundle of people up to the surface. It was getting dark by now but, looking at them closely, Sacaibou was dismayed to find himself with six ugly bad-tempered little men and women. "Oh – Rairou has got muddled up," he thought, frowning, as he watched them setting off.

But then he felt the cotton line torn out of his hands. Rairou's voice, coming up from below, said: "That's my revenge – now it's too late, you'll never be able to cover the earth just with good people." He gave a triumphant laugh. "There'll always be all sorts!" Then Rairou became silent.

Sacaibou sat down on a stone in the twilight. He thought very hard about what had happened.

How the world almost came to an end

(Pamarís, Amazon River)

The Pamarís live on the edges of lakes. Their huts are built on legs.

They tell how, long ago, a great noise was heard both above and below ground. The sun and the moon became first red and then blue and then yellow. The people were very frightened. But the wild animals came and mixed with them without being afraid.

A month later the noise began again, only it was even louder and this time there was darkness in the sky and on the earth. Rain fell day and night and the thunder did not stop either. Many people ran off and were never seen again.

The waters rose. Soon only the tops of the trees were not covered. Many people climbed up them but gradually they all died of hunger.

All except two: Ouassou and Sofara, a man and a woman. Once the waters dropped they climbed down. There was no trace of the other people, not even their bones.

The man and the woman had children and slowly the earth became peopled again. But the closest descendants of Ouassou and Sofara – that's the

Pamarís – have ever since lived in huts on legs, just in case the waters should one day rise again.

Life and death of a sun

(Juruna people of Brazil)

The Sun lived far away, with his wife and three children. They spoke their own language. Near their house was a great stone and, in it, a deep hole which was always full of water. It was the Sun's trap: many animals went there to drink but, when they put their heads in the hole, they found they could not get them out again . . . and soon the Sun came and killed them and ate them.

A young Juruna, out hunting, saw the water. "I'll drink there," he said to himself. He put a hand in to scoop up some water – and found it was stuck fast. The man had to stay there all night. In the morning, seeing the Sun coming and guessing that he had been caught in his trap, the Juruna was so afraid that his heart stopped beating for a while.

"He looks dead already," said the Sun to himself. So he just dropped the man into his basket along with some animals he had caught earlier that morning. The Sun reached his home again in the evening. He hung his basket on a tree near his house. In the night the young man climbed down and set off back to his village.

Next morning the Sun was very cross. "I was looking forward to eating a man!" he bellowed. The Sun picked up his club: "Go off and kill him, wherever he's got to!" And he threw the club into the air. It hurtled away, but hit a deer by mistake.

So the Sun had to chase the young Juruna himself. As he saw the great light getting nearer and nearer, the man jumped into a hollow tree. The Sun's club got to it before his master – it thumped away at the trunk of the tree.

"You're hopeless!" roared the Sun. "Get out of the way!" The Sun quickly cut a stick and started poking at the man inside the tree. The Juruna was wounded all over but he would not come out.

Luckily for him, it was getting late, so the Sun had to go home for the night. But, before he went, the Sun covered up the entrance hole with a great stone. "We'll get him out tomorrow," he said to his club as they went off.

The young man found he could not lift the stone. He was afraid that his last night had come. But then he heard all sorts of grunts and squeaks outside. The animals had heard the Sun bellowing away and had come to see what was going on. Roundabout the hollow tree there were now tapirs, wild pigs, monkeys, agoutis, pacas and other animals of the forest.

The man cried out: "Please help me to get out of here!"

A tapir at once started chewing a hole in the side of

the tree. When his teeth began to break, an agouti took his place. Both the tapirs and the agoutis spend their days gnawing with their strong teeth. The other animals helped as best they could. The hole got bigger and bigger. . . .

The Sun was back at dawn – but the Juruna was then just reaching home. He told his family all about his adventure.

After three days, he said: "I'm going out to look for coconuts."

"But the Sun will see you and kill you!" his mother said at once. She burst into tears, asking him not to go out.

"No, he won't know me," replied the young man. Early the next morning, he cut off his long hair and painted his body with the bluish-black juice of the genipap plant. He climbed up a palm-tree and began cutting off the big brown nuts.

The Sun now came over the horizon. Just another monkey, he thought to himself at first. But then he *did* recognize the Juruna. "Now you are caught!" he shouted triumphantly. Armed with his huge club, he stood waiting at the bottom of the palm.

The man thought hard. Then he shouted down: "Look, I've cut all these coconuts, it's a pity to waste them – please catch them."

"All right," agreed the Sun, who liked coconuts too.

The Juruna threw down a small bundle and the Sun caught them. Then the man dropped a huge netful of the nuts. It hit the Sun in the chest and crushed him so that he fell dead on the ground.

Slowly his light faded. The earth grew dark. The club turned into a snake – the sort the Juruna now call the *uandaré* or "sun's club" – and slithered away into the forest. The Sun's blood spread over the earth, turning into ants, centipedes, snakes and other dangerous creatures that crawl along the ground. There were so many that the young man had to go from tree to tree to get home safely.

It was now like night although it was the middle of the day. Frightened and bewildered, the Juruna's family sat silently in their dark hut. "What has happened?" asked his mother as he came in.

"I've killed the Sun," replied the man.

The woman replied sadly: "But what will we all do now? Nobody can work or hunt or fish! We'll starve to death in the dark. You have done us a great harm by killing the Sun."

All the family now wept, as did their neighbours and other people away across the world. There seemed no hope for there was nothing they could do.

At the Sun's house also there was sadness. It was dark there too and the Sun's wife said: "Your father must be dead – he liked to kill things and now somebody has killed him. So now we have nobody to hunt for us." She looked at the three boys. "One of you will have to take his place."

So the eldest set off up into the sky. He wore the feathered head-dress that the sun always wears – but, as the time came for dawn over the Jurunas' land, the boy found the head-dress was getting so hot that he came down again. The world passed another day in darkness.

The second boy went up a little higher but the heat was too much for him too. Another day passed in darkness.

The third boy did manage to put up with the heat. But he had to go across the sky so fast, in order to get the journey over, that the people on the earth had no time to work or hunt or fish.

So when the young sun came home his mother said: "You did well. But in future you must go more slowly; you can rest in the middle of the day, when you're at the top."

The boy did as she said, so that the Juruna and all the rest of the world's peoples were able to go back to their normal lives. Only the new Sun's mother was sorry, as she would now never have her youngest son at home during the day.

Kahukura and the fishing-net

(Maoris of New Zealand)

Kahukura is the hero of many Maori stories. During
his travels he landed on a beach which he found was
covered with fish guts. He pulled up his canoe.

"Somebody has just been fishing here, or the tide
would have washed all this mess away," he thought.
"But that's strange – there aren't any rushes. . . ."
Kahukura's people always spread rushes over the
floors of their canoes, changing them for fresh ones
wherever they landed. "The fairies must have been
fishing here!" he said aloud, in surprise.

That night Kahukura came back. He had hidden
his canoe and now crept quietly over the rocky
ground behind the beach. And some figures were
indeed fishing, by the light of the moon. A canoe was
just being launched. But what especially surprised
Kahukura was the strange thing the figures had
stretched out between them: it was a net. This was
unknown to the Maoris, each of whom fished with a
line and a hook.

One end of the net was fixed to the shore. The
canoe paddled out in a great curve, letting go the net
as it did so, until it had come back to the beach again,

landing further along. "Here you are!" shouted a figure, throwing a rope to one of the fairies who had stayed on the shore.

"Now! Pull!" cried those on the land, heaving away. The paddlers jumped out and pulled too.

Kahukura helped. He was short and fair, rather like the fairies, so that in the near-darkness they did not see that he was a human. The jumping fish glinted in the light of the moon. The net got caught on a rock in the middle of the bay but the fairies quickly paddled out and freed it. At last they had hauled the net into the shore . . . and at once the beach was covered with leaping mackerel.

But the sky was already a little lighter. The fairies began to work faster. Now they were gutting the fish. "Quickly, or it'll be dawn before we've finished!" cried one.

They began threading the fish on to strings. Kahukura made a sliding knot on the end of his string. As soon as a fairy came to take up his line of fish, the knot rolled off the end and all the fish fell to the ground.

"Oh, dear, oh, dear!" exclaimed another fairy. "Here, let me do it for you. . . ."

But as soon as the fairy had gone back to his own work, Kahukura altered the knot – and when another fairy came for the fish they all slid off again!

At that moment the first ray of sunlight fell on the sands. "Oh!" cried out all the fairies together. And then they saw Kahukura's face, with its tattoo marks.

"Look – a man!" the fairies shouted. Catching up their strings of fish, they ran off into the hills, leaving behind the net and their canoes.

With the sun rising, Kahukura found himself alone on the silent beach. First he looked carefully at the long narrow boats: they were made of flax stalks. Then he walked over to the heaped net: it was made of knotted rushes. Kahukura made very sure he would remember how the net had been made.

Since then the Maoris have fished with nets. And when they want to say that a piece of work has been done badly they say it reminds them of the knot on Kahukura's string.

The bird of stone

(Maoris of New Zealand)

Kupe was one of the first men to explore the northern island. On the prow of his canoe travelled two birds. The wood pigeon came to seek out the food which the forests held, such as nuts and fruits. The shag's task was to explore the dangerous waterways ahead of Kupe's canoe.

The shag tested the currents and the tides by settling on the water and trying itself out against them. Then it would report back to Kupe on how strong they were and on when they were slack or in flood.

One day Kawau-a-toru, as the brave shag was called, was talking to some other sea-birds which lived on the great island.

"We're going up the east coast next," said the shag. His wings were spread out as he stood on the rock, drying them in the way shags always do.

"Then you must take great care of the channel between the little island of Rangitoto and the mainland," replied another bird, "for it runs like a great river."

Kawau-a-toru enjoyed its struggles with the sea and so, flying on ahead of Kupe's canoe, it at once went up to Rangitoto. Reaching the channel, the shag heard the sound of the water racing between the two shores. Beating low across the surface on its powerful wings, it first flew the length of the channel.

Then it turned and came back, to try itself against the tide-race. Kawau-a-toru dipped a wing in the rippling water. But it found itself at once dragged along by the current. The shag, struggling to fly, could not get free. Gradually it tired . . . and its other wing touched the hissing surface and was gripped in its turn by the water.

Kawau-a-toru the brave shag lost this contest. It never returned to Kupe's canoe. The Maoris say it was turned into stone – into the rock now in the middle of the Rangitoto channel. And in fact Kawau-a-toru thus goes on with his work, for the rock always reminds those in canoes of the dangers of the tide-race.

The friends of the tree

(Maoris of New Zealand)

In the forest stood a fine straight tree. Nobody knows
what sort it was – there were so many types of trees in
the Maoris' ancient forests. Ratu, the hero of many
stories, decided to make a canoe out of the tree.

So he sharpened his axe and, without another
moment's thought about it, chopped the fine tree
down. But when he came back the next morning the
tree was standing again. The dew glistened on its
leaves, the sun shone on its rough bark.

Surprised and annoyed, Ratu thoughtlessly took up
his axe and once more chopped the tree down. This
time he lopped off all the branches too.

But the next morning there was the tree standing
up once more. On the leaves there were insects, on its
branches were all sorts of birds. The wind sang
through the tree on its way through the forest.

Ratu snatched up his axe and ran angrily at the
tree. For the third time he cut it down.

But he came back at dawn the next day. Moving
quietly through the forest, he drew close to the tree
he wanted for his canoe. To his surprise, he heard a

great deal of noise ahead of him. It was the buzzing
and fluttering of the wings of swarms of bees, beetles,
birds and other forest creatures. Ratu could hear
some of the birds singing too.

Then, peering through the bushes, he saw a sur-
prising sight. The fallen tree was surrounded by the
many creatures which lived in or on it – and they
were putting back its branches, leaves and bark in
their right places.

The tree was already complete again. Ratu saw the
spririts of the forest appear and start to pull it
upright. But his anger took hold of him at this and he
ran out of his hiding-place, shouting:

"Stop that, it's my tree!"

The animals and spirits of the forest turned
towards Ratu and, with one voice, replied: "And who
gave you permission to kill one of our trees?"

The blind boy and
the loon

(Chugach Eskimos)

One of the boys in an Eskimo family had been born
blind. Now he was just eight years old. Although he
could not see, he often went out in his father's canoe
to help him fish. At other times he worked with his
mother, softening up the sealskins for making clothes.
He shared other jobs with his brothers and sisters.

One midsummer's day the family set up their camp
on a beach, beside the sea. There were icebergs
floating on the water. This was the day when the sun
never goes down in the far north.

After supper the blind boy slowly wandered away
up a track on to some higher ground. Soon he heard
the sound of waves on a rocky shore and guessed he
had reached a lake.

Across the water came the call of a loon: "Kkaarr-
arr! Kkaarr-arr!" The loon is a grey-brown diving
bird with a long neck and a crest on top of its head.

Feeling the warmth of the sun on his face, the boy
stood silently on the water's edge. The bird's cry grew
louder and louder. Then the boy heard a rustling
and, stretching out his hand, felt the soft feathers of
the loon's body – he could always recognize things

with his hands, whether it was a wriggling worm that he was putting on his father's fishing line or the silky skin of a seal which his mother would make into a jacket.

The blind boy climbed on to the loon's back. At once the bird stepped into the water. It swam towards the middle of the lake. The boy put his arms around the bird's long neck – just as it dived.

Down the two went, through floating plants and startled fish. Deep in the dark water, the loon began to swim round and round the lake. Once, twice, three times, four times, five times. The water streamed past the boy's face – he had never known such a feeling before. Now the loon swam upwards.

The boy felt the water becoming lighter. Then the shining surface was stretched like a skin above them and the loon's long neck burst through it, so that they were out in the sunlight again.

Only this time it was not just the warmth which the boy could feel. The sun's light was so bright that he had to hide his face in the loon's feathers. A few moments later he felt the bird's feet touch the shore.

The boy jumped off the loon's back. In front of him were the pebbles and rocks of the lake's beach, with some tiny green plants amongst them. The boy looked at them in delight. He could see, for the first time in his life. Then he heard the loon's wings beating and, turning round, saw the bird was flying across the lake again. The boy ran down the slopes to his family's camp.

The others were out on the sea, fishing from their two canoes. The boy raced into the big tent, opened a bag and pulled out a small apron covered with rows of white sea-shells. It had taken him a long time to sew the shells on the piece of skin – for a moment he stopped to look at it.

When he got back to the lake, he called the loon: "Kkaarr-arr! Kkaarr-arr!" This was the bird's own cry.

Soon the loon was flying back across the lake to the rocky beach. The boy gently tied the apron of shells around the bird's neck.

Then he watched the loon fly away again across the water. The low sun shone on the bird's white front. The Eskimos who live in this land now say that's why all loons have white chests.

The otter makes a bargain

(Chugach Eskimos)

All the animals were once shared out between the Spirit of the Land and the Spirit of the Sea. It was a long task. The otter found itself left until last.

"It'll live in the water," said the Spirit of the Sea.

"No," replied the Spirit of the Land. "It must live on the land."

At this the two spirits caught hold of the otter by its head and its tail – and pulled. Until then the poor

animal had only a very short tail, but now it began to stretch.

"Please let me go!" cried the otter. "I'll spend my life with both of you, I promise."

This is why the otters have ever since spent part of their time swimming and fishing and the rest living in dens on the land.

Go where the stick points

(Eskimos of the Arctic)

The chief of the village of Na-ki-a-ki-a-mute was a
short strong man who was very much respected by
the people for his skill as a hunter – his aim was good,
he could run very fast and he never tired, no matter
how long the chase lasted. He lived with his wife.
They had no children.

Among their neighbours were an old woman and
her granddaughter. They lived in a tiny house and
were very poor because they had nobody to hunt for
them. But the chief gave them a share of the food he
brought home. The little girl used to fetch water
every day for his wife, filling the skin by dipping it in
a hole in the ice which covered a lake behind the
beach where they all lived. The chief's wife was very
fond of the girl.

One day the chief went out to hunt in his canoe as
usual. He harpooned a seal. It dived but the chief had
a line tied to the harpoon and on its end was a skin
full of air which floated. So he knew where the seal
was and, when at last it had to come up to breathe, he
killed it with a second harpoon. The man laid the
seal across the back of his canoe and set off home.

"My wife will be pleased; it's a good fat one," he thought as he paddled back through the floating icebergs.

As he walked up the beach towards his house, he was surprised not to see any smoke coming from it. He went inside but his wife was not there. It had been snowing the night before; the chief walked right round the house but the only tracks he could find were his own going to the sea, though by the door there were some marks in the snow which were strange to him.

Very worried, the chief now called on the other villagers but nobody had seen his wife that day. The man went back to his house. He soon became very miserable and would not talk to anyone. He neither ate nor slept. During the day he sat outside his house with his weapons around him, looking so fierce and angry that all the people were afraid to go near him.

But after a while the old woman who lived near by said to her granddaughter: "We can't let him go on like this. You go and bring him here to eat with us. His wife loved you, I'm sure he won't be unkind to you."

The girl was very frightened. She went shyly up to the chief, who was sitting outside his house as usual, and, taking his hand, said: "Please come to our house, my grandma is cooking a meal."

To her surprise and relief, the man's face broke into a smile. He stood up and walked back with her to the little house. Soon he was eating a big meal of fish and seal-meat; he found he was so hungry, as he had not eaten for so long, that the little girl went off to get more food from his own house.

While they were waiting for her to come back, the old woman said: "Now I want to repay your kindness in the past – for I think I can help you now. First, you must make a strong staff out of drifted-up wood. Then tie these charms to it."

She handed the chief several small animals and human faces carved in ivory, together with a bunch of feathers from the birds which lived on the sea round-about the village. The man was very grateful.

The woman went on: "In the evening put the stick upright in the ground in front of your house – make sure it's in really firmly so that the wind can't blow it over. Then, in the morning, go where the stick points. Use it as a guide and you'll find your wife again."

The little girl was soon back with more meat. The chief ate until he was full and then went home. Quickly he made the staff, tied on the charms and set it up in the snow. Then he rolled himself up in the huge skin of a white bear and went to sleep.

In the morning, after his first meal and rest for a long time, he felt strong again. At once going outside, he found the stick was leaning over towards the north. He pulled it up and, taking nothing else, set off across the snow.

The chief had to climb across a range of mountains and then swim over an icy river, travelling without stopping for two days and two nights. Then, putting the stick in the ground, he slept under a rock for a few hours. When he woke, the stick was leaning well over, again towards the north.

He now journeyed across vast plains of snow and then over the frozen sea, this time for three days and three nights. Then he dug a shelter in the snow and slept a little while. In the morning the stick lay almost on the ground. "My wife is very near . . ." the man thought to himself.

That day he spent marching northwards through a blizzard and the night in crossing an ice-field broken up by deep holes. At noon the next day the dark red sun rose for a few moments above the horizon. "The colour of blood," thought the chief, as the snow turned crimson.

Suddenly, ahead, he saw a larger ice-house than he had ever seen in his life. Outside it were four posts on which hung a huge bird-skin. The chief hid behind some tiny willow trees, lying flat on the snow. After a while a very tall man came out, put on the skin and flew away over the sea.

The chief grasped his staff and ran to the ice-house. He crawled quickly along the entrance tunnel . . . and there, sitting sadly by a fire of seal blubber, was his wife. They embraced each other.

The woman said: "I knew you'd come in the end!"

The man asked: "What happened?"

"That terrible bird carried me here in his claws."

"So that's why there were no footprints," said the

chief, nodding his head. Then he took her hand. "Come on, we must leave at once."

"No," said his wife. "The bird hasn't gone far today – I've a plan. . . ."

Taking some meat as he was now hungry again, the chief went back to his hiding-place. He covered himself with snow so that he would not be seen.

Almost at once the great wings of the bird were heard beating across the sky. The chief, watching through the willow trees, saw the shadowy figure diving down towards the ice-house. In one claw it held a seal and in the other a walrus. The tall man stepped out of the bird-skin.

But the chief's wife, who had heard the sound of the wings too, crawled out of the tunnel and, standing up, said: "Oh, not seal and walrus meat *again*!" She began to cry. "I've had enough of this sort of food. Please get me a white whale and a hump-back whale, they're so much better to eat."

Her captor stared at her for a moment and then, frowning, again put on the skin. The great bird vanished into the darkness.

At once the woman ran across to her husband. They set off together over the dark and dangerous ice-field. By the morning the woman had tired but her husband took her on his back. The blizzard raged all that day. They slept in a shelter they dug in the snow.

The next morning, just as they were crossing the frozen sea, the bird caught them up. It held a dead

whale in each claw. "Once I've taken these back to my ice-house I shall come after you . . . and kill both of you." The great bird flew away northwards.

The man and woman crossed the snow plains and spent the night under the rock. The next morning they reached the great river.

"I can't swim," said the woman.

"I'll take you on my back," replied her husband, though he was now tiring too.

But at that moment they heard the beating of wings in the distance.

"Quick!" cried the chief. "Let's go into that little cave in the bank, it's too small for the bird to follow us inside."

Just in time, they ran into the cave – the entrance was at once darkened by the body and wings of the bird. It gave a furious cry, but then said: "You won't escape me – now I shall drown you."

Looking out, the chief and his wife saw a huge wing set right across the river. The water began to rise . . . they heard the bird laugh. . . .

The woman said: "Your father was an *angakoks*, you must do as he would have done." An *angakoks* was a magician.

"Yes . . ." agreed the chief. And after thinking hard for a few moments he said: "I can remember one of his rhymes – I'll try it."

Three times he said:
   "Kluk-a-luk
   Muk-a-luk
   Puk-a-luk."

This meant: "Freeze hard or you'll run dry." It was in fact October, the time when the rivers start to freeze. Now it was a race between the rising water and the cold which suddenly fell over the river. . . .

The man and woman in the cave heard a cry of rage from the great bird. Through the entrance they saw it was struggling to free its wing from the water. But it was too late: the wing was frozen into the river.

The chief broke a great icicle from the cave's roof and ran outside. He raced across the ice of the freezing river and killed the bird with a thrust of his ice-spear.

The winter brought great happiness to both the man and his wife and to the old woman and her granddaughter. They now all lived together. The body of the enormous bird gave them food for the whole winter. And, added to the old woman's charms, which had worked so well, there was now a huge feather.

The devil's violin

(Gipsies of Transylvania)

Deep in the forest there was a small house in which lived a girl with her father, mother and four brothers. They had an ordinary life: the man cut and sold wood, his wife looked after their animals while their four sons and their daughter helped them with the work.

But one day a huntsman rode past. He wore a green cap and brown woollen jacket and trousers and across his back were slung a bow and quiver of arrows. The girl, in a long blue dress, her hair in a pigtail, saw him go by and she at once fell in love with him.

Soon the man rode past again. The girl spoke to him: "Good morning! Are you going far?"

The hunter simply nodded and rode on. The girl felt a little sad at this.

The next day the young man again came past the little house. The girl, sitting on a wall, made sure he heard her singing. She could sing beautifully. But the hunter just looked the other way, slowly riding past. Now the girl wept.

That night she went to a clearing in the woods and asked the devil to help her. The next morning there was an old mirror in the fork of a tree there.

About noon the sound of the hunter's horse was heard through the forest. The girl took the mirror and stood with it on the track. But as soon as the man saw it, he raised his arm like a shield – as if he knew where it had come from – and turned his horse round, galloping away. And now the girl wept and wept, for she had failed to make him look in the mirror. If he had done so then he would have been caught, for the people of the forest knew the power of the devil's mirror.

So that night the girl once more went off alone into the forest. Reaching the clearing, she lit a fire and stood the mirror in the tree where she had found it. Then she called on the devil again.

Slowly the mirror lost the reflection of the flames, instead getting darker. And, just as slowly, it grew larger until it was as big as the girl. Then, in it, she saw a shadowy figure.

A voice said: "To get your way you must give me your father, mother and four brothers."

The girl willingly gave them to the devil. The father was turned into a wooden box, the brothers into four strings each giving a different sound, the mother into a bow; and inside the great mirror, the girl saw the shadowy figure was now playing this violin – something she had never seen before, for it was the first violin ever made. The girl saw her

mother's long grey hair had been used to string the bow.

The next day the girl sat outside the empty house and played that violin. She played all day and all night, playing the many tunes which the devil had taught her. And on the third day she heard the sound of hooves. . . . It was the huntsman, still in his green hat and brown jacket and trousers . . . slowly he rode through the trees, as if he came against his will. . . . The girl, in her long blue dress, ran to greet him.

The young man had come to live with her in the little house. The girl was so happy – and so perhaps was the young man . . . the gipsy story-tellers do not seem to know how he felt.

But on the ninth day, as twilight was falling, the little mirror on the wall of the house began to grow dark. The girl and the man watched as it became larger and larger. A shadowy figure now beckoned to them from within. Slowly, against their wills, the girl and the man disappeared into the mirror.

One day – again the story-tellers do not say how long after – a poor gipsy was passing by the little house. It was now in ruins. The gipsy went in through the gaping doorway and, on the overgrown floor, found a violin. He picked it up and took it away.

This was how the gipsies first came to play the violin – and from this very special violin, with its story of joy and sadness, comes the power of the gipsies' music to make people both laugh and cry.

The little duck and the big water-rat

(Noongahburrah people of Australia)

One little duck was much more daring than the rest, often swimming away alone down the creek.

"Look out!" the others would cry. "Mulloon the water-devil will catch you!"

But it was Biggoon, a huge water-rat, who caught her one day, as she was eating away at a bank of green weed. The rat said: "You're going to be my wife."

The little duck replied: "But my tribe already has a mate for me."

But the rat only answered: "Don't worry, I won't hurt you – unless you try to escape. Then I'll stick my little spears into you!" The water-rats have sharp points on the heels of their back feet.

"My people will come and attack you," said the little duck, trying not to give in.

"No, they won't," the rat replied with a grin. "Because they'll just think that Mulloon has got you. And anyway, if they do come, I've got my little spears. . . ."

So the poor duck had to stay all day in Biggoon's hole in the bank of the creek. He would only let her out at night, because then the other ducks were not swimming about as they were afraid that Mulloon would catch them. Days went by and Biggoon decided that the little duck had settled down to her new life. So he went back to sleeping all day, as he had always done.

But as soon as the little duck saw he was no longer watching her, she crept out of the hole and swam quietly away upstream. Then, once she was out of sight, she flew into the air . . . and was soon home again.

The rest of her people were very pleased to see her. All the young ducks were told never to swim downstream.

Now it was the time when ducks lay eggs and soon the hollow trees and the *mirrieh* bushes were full of feather-lined nests. The little duck laid two eggs too. Soon the first chicks were being led down to the

water and the creek was covered with big ducks teaching their young how to swim and to get their food.

Suddenly there was a great noise. Everybody was looking at the little duck. She had only two chicks and they were covered in soft fur instead of feathers and had four feet instead of two. And, though they did have ordinary ducks' bills and webbed feet, they had no wings and their back heels had points on them like little spears.

After a lot of excited talking, the chief of the ducks spoke for the whole tribe: "You'll have to take them away from here. They're more like Biggoon than us. One day they'll be so big that they'll eat us. If you don't take them off then we'll have to kill them before it's too late."

So the unlucky little duck had to leave her home again. "Where shall I go?" she asked herself. "If I go downstream then Biggoon will catch us all. He will shut me up again and perhaps kill my chicks because they've got duck-bills and webbed feet. Oh, dear, nobody will want us!"

So she swam upstream with her chicks, into the mountains. The creek got smaller and smaller until it was just a little stream. Here the three of them stopped.

The chicks grew quickly. But, as the days went by, they wanted less and less to do with their mother, for they lived in a different way: they ate different foods, slept in other places and so on.

The little duck felt lonely and miserable, far from her people and her home, or her *noorumbah* as the Noongahburrah call home in their language. So, too sad to even get herself her food any longer, she died.

But the mountain streams are now full of animals like the ones she first mothered. They are called platypuses and people still think them strange because they have a duck's beak, dark-brown fur and webbed feet with little spears on their back heels.

Goolayyahlee the pelican

(Noongahburrah people of Australia)

In this corner of Australia, where the Noongahburrah live, fishing used always to be done by making a wall of strong grass and creeper right across the creek. The people then went into the water and drove the fish against the wall. Then they picked them out and threw them up on to the banks. Sometimes they would put the wall across a small side-creek when it was in flood, so that the fish were left behind in the mud when the waters dropped. But it did take a long time to build walls like those and they did not last very long. The idea of using a net came to men in a very strange way. . . .

Goolayyahlee the pelican was a great magician. He had the first net but nobody knew where he kept it. When he and his family were about to go fishing, he would say to his children: "Now off you go and get eurah sticks for the ends of the net." The *eurah* was a small droopy tree covered in big yellow-white bell-flowers. It grew near water.

The little pelicans always came back to find the net already laid out on the ground. Beside it there was a small fire of twigs onto which Goolayyahlee was

58

throwing *eurah* leaves. Then they all held the net in the smoke. The little *eurah* tree was sacred: using it for the sticks and to smoke the net helped to make sure that the fishing would be a success.

And the net really made fishing easy. Two pelicans held it while the others chased the fish down the creek into it. Then they all had a good meal.

One day one of Goolayyahlee's children decided to find out where the net was kept. So, instead of going off with the others to get the *eurah* sticks, he hid behind a rock near the camp. To his surprise, he saw Goolayyahlee do some very strange things: he stretched his neck, waggled his head, stood on tiptoe, hiccupped, stretched his neck again – and then out of his huge bill came the end of the net . . . gradually it heaped up on the ground in front of him!

Of course everybody soon knew where the net was kept and so Goolayyahlee, anyway fed up with having to keep swallowing it, decided to show all the other tribes how to make nets:

"You strip the bark off a *noongah* tree, take off the hard outside and then chew the inside until it's soft enough to be made into a sort of string. It's from this that you make your net – you just knot the string up into squares." Though Goolayyahlee, being a great magician, just swallowed the soft part of the bark and the string and then the net just made itself inside him . . . but he never told anybody how *this* was done.

The Noongahburrah people now say that if you watch pelicans fishing you'll see that they sweep their long yellow-pouched bills through the water as if they were pulling on a net – where other fishing birds dip their bills straight into the water. The fish go down into the nets inside the pelicans . . . the name Goolayyahlee means "he who has a net".

Why the owl has such huge eyes

(Native people of Australia)

Weemullee the Owl and Willanjee the Hurricane lived out in the desert. They were very good friends, sharing the same camp, hunting together, cooking and eating and sleeping at the same fire. In fact they spent all their time together.

There was just one thing that upset Weemullee about his friend: he could never see Willanjee. You might say it didn't matter whether he ever set eyes on the Hurricane. But there it was, Weemullee had got it into his head that he wanted to see Willanjee.

"Why aren't you like the rest of us?" Weemullee would ask. "You could change yourself."

"No, certainly not," Willanjee always replied. He did not like being asked this and was always silent for a long time afterwards.

As on most days, on the day of this story the sun was up early, waking the Owl and the Hurricane. "Shall we go hunting?" said Weemullee.

Willanjee yawned and said: "I could eat a whole kangaroo, I'm so hungry – let's go off at once."

They went across the desert towards some trees. Weemullee carried his spear under his wing while

Willanjee had his on his shoulder. Of course the Hurricane was invisible, but Weemullee could tell where he was because of the spear moving steadily along beside him.

"Look, there's a kangaroo, by that big gum tree," said Weemullee, pointing ahead. "I'll fly round in a circle and chase him towards you. . . ."

Willanjee, his spear now ready in its thrower, hid behind a rock. Soon the kangaroo came leaping towards him. Behind, flapping his wings and hooting frighteningly, flew Weemullee.

Willanjee rose up from behind the rock and flung his spear. It sped through the air and the kangaroo fell to the ground. Weemullee and Willanjee gave cries of triumph.

They hunted all day. By evening they had also caught several iguana lizards and two black ducks.

Just as they were thinking of going back to their camp, Weemullee caught a fat young opossum in a hollow in a tree.

"Throw it down," said Willanjee.

The owl did so.

Willanjee caught it and flung it over his shoulder with the other dead animals. Weemullee picked up his own load and together they went home.

After supper, Willanjee said: "Well, that *was* good." He threw a last kangaroo bone on the fire.

"Time to turn in," said Weemullee, yawning.

So they rolled their skin blankets round themselves and lay down by the fire. But Weemullee could not

sleep for wondering if, perhaps, he might be able to see Willanjee while he was asleep.

It was a quiet night and so the Owl had to move very carefully to avoid waking the Hurricane. He crept over and, his eyes opened very wide, unrolled the end of Willanjee's cover. . . .

But a terrible thing happened: Willanjee thought he was being attacked and he flung aside his skin and burst into the air, tearing up the bushes, scattering the still-glowing wood of the fire, sending the dry dusty red earth and dead leaves whirling up into the sky. Weemullee was blown into a tree, dragged through its branches, so that lots of his feathers were torn out, and then thrown on to the open plain. In the end the Owl managed to catch hold of a strong acacia tree and there he waited until the Hurricane had gone off across the desert.

Willanjee too was very tired and, when he realized it had been Weemullee's curiosity which had woken him up, he was very cross and never came back to their camp. Nobody knows where he now lives, except for the six winds, who will tell nobody. Nor does Willanjee speak properly any more, but just roars and howls.

Weemullee did manage to get his feathers tidied up again. But he has ever since looked out at the world through the big round eyes with which he had been hoping to see Willanjee on that terrible night.

The shield and the shell

(Native people of Australia)

Yams – they're roots like giant potatoes – grow wild in parts of Australia. Oolah, taking her three children, went out on to a plain with her digging stick. As the morning passed, so her heap of yams grew bigger.

When they were close to a patch of *mirrieh* bushes, out jumped a man called Wayambeh – and seized Oolah and her children. "I'm going to take you back to my camp to be my wife!" he said.

Oolah and her children shouted and screamed and struggled. The sight of his spears frightened them, and Wayambeh was too strong for them.

In the end they had to go back to the man's camp. It was on the edge of a creek. The other people there were very surprised. One asked: "Did her tribe give her to you, Wayambeh?"

"No," he replied. "I stole her."

Another man then said: "You did wrong, her people will soon come after her."

"We had a wife for you here," added a third. "You'll pay for this."

The second man was soon proved right. "Here they come!" he shouted from on top of a rock.

Marching across the plain were the men of Oolah's tribe. One of Wayambeh's friends cried: "They've neither women nor branches of peace with them – look out, Wayambeh, they're coming to fight."

As they drew closer, another man, up a tree, shouted: "Yes, they've got their fighting paint on and they're carrying spears and boomerangs!"

The chief of Wayambeh's tribe now said to him: "This is nothing to do with us. You'll have to look after yourself."

Wayambeh had two huge shields and now he fixed one on his front and the other on his back. Then, taking his spears, he went out to face his attackers. His own tribe watched from their camp. When the men were still some way off, Wayambeh shouted a challenge to them.

At once the attackers flung their spears and boomerangs. But, as these showered on to him, Wayambeh quickly drew his head, arms and legs in within the two great shields. The weapons clattered and rattled on the shields, then fell to the ground.

Wayambeh, unhurt, put his head and then his arms and legs out again. Once more he dared Oolah's tribesmen to attack him and once more the rain of spears and boomerangs did him no harm.

But now the men were running towards him. Wayambeh turned, hoping to escape, but found himself on the edge of the creek. So he dived in.

The men from Oolah's tribe stood, spears ready, on the bank. But, to their surprise, Wayambeh did not come up again.

After a while, one man pointed: "Look – what's that?"

The sun shone through the water on to a strange creature sitting on the bottom. A man tried to stick his spear into it but the animal at once drew its head and limbs in under its huge shell – and the spear did not harm it. Then the creature swam away under the water.

"That was Wayambeh!" exclaimed the men in surprise.

Since that day there have been turtles in the creeks of Australia.

The day the pygmy put on a tail

(Pygmies of the Ituri Forest, Congo)

The Bambuti pygmies spend a lot of their time hunting. One man had been wandering through the forest all day in search of food. Suddenly he found himself looking down through the trees on to a village of chimpanzees. Some time ago there had been bad feelings between the pygmies and the chimpanzees because the men had stolen the secret of how to grow bananas from the monkeys.

But, tired and hungry, the pygmy decided he would go into the village and ask for food. The monkeys were very friendly and gave the pygmy a big bunch of delicious bananas. As it was getting cold, they asked the pygmy to sit down with them round their fire. The warmth and the dancing flames pleased the pygmy very much – his people did not know how to make fire.

The man spent the night sleeping amongst the monkeys close to the flames. In the morning he set off home – but he was careful to mark the path so that he could find his way back to the chimpanzee village.

A few days later, the pygmy came again. It was the afternoon and the older monkeys were all working in

the banana trees. But the children knew the pygmy and so, as usual, they gave him some bananas and asked him to sit down with them.

But as he walked ahead of them towards the fire they all suddenly burst out laughing. "Look at that!" cried one of the little monkeys.

Hanging down behind him, fixed to his waist cloth, the pygmy had a long tail made of plaited-bark string. The chimpanzee children thought this so funny that they could not stop laughing. The pygmy just grinned and sat down.

After a while, a little monkey said: "Look out, your *murumba* (that was his tail) is going to catch fire!"

The pygmy just shrugged his shoulders. "It's far too long anyway," he replied. He went on eating his bananas. But from time to time, out of the corner of his eye, he did look at his tail. He seemed to want it to go into the fire. . . .

At length the tail's tip was smouldering. The pygmy jumped up and, without even saying goodbye, ran off.

The little chimpanzees felt there was something wrong about this and they raced into the trees to tell their mothers and fathers. One of these at once guessed what had happened: "The pygmy has stolen our fire!"

So the chimpanzees swung through the trees after the running pygmy. But the man knew the way better than they did – and, by the time they had reached his camp, there were fires alight everywhere.

The chimpanzees were very cross and tried to make the pygmies give back the fire. But these refused to do so.

This made the monkeys so upset that they decided to go far away from all men, into the deepest forest. There they now live, with neither their own banana trees nor fire.

Why the Efe are not afraid of lightning

(Pygmies of the Ituri Forest, Congo)

A band of pygmies was out on an elephant hunt. Although they were the smallest men in all the world, with their spears, poisoned arrows and traps they could kill the biggest of all the animals. But sometimes they would get lost in their own forests, these were so thick and huge.

The band of pygmies found themselves on a great mountain which they had never seen before. A wide track which seemed to have been burnt through the forest led them to a huge hut.

There was nobody in sight. The Efe men stared at the hut. The walls and roof were made of gigantic trees which had been split in half down the middle. They would have been so heavy that no man could have possibly lifted them into place.

Then, far away across the sky, they saw a streak of light. Quickly it drew nearer.

A pygmy cried out: "I know – this is the house of the Lightning!"

They were all very frightened but it was too late to hide, for the Lightning was already overhead. Seeing the men around his house, he was very cross – and he

drew back his arm, about to hurl one of his great shafts of light at the pygmies.

But, just in time, his daughter caught him up. "See," she said to the Lightning, "they're carrying elephant spears – they must be hunters."

There was a terrible silence while the Lightning thought about this . . . and then he lowered his arm and smiled at the pygmies. "Would you help me to kill some elephants which keep breaking into my garden?" he asked them.

Nothing was easier for the pygmies and, soon, they had hunted and killed the elephants. The Lightning was very pleased. He gave the men presents.

"Just follow me and I'll show you the way back to your camp," said the Lightning.

Soon the pygmies were home again. After saying goodbye, the Lightning and his daughter went off across the sky to take part in a storm far away. Ever since that day the pygmies have been friends with the lightning. You can see this from the way that they build their huts against trees – although most people would tell them that the Lightning usually strikes a tall tree rather than an open space.

Kara-tuma, the cow and the sorghum

(Bushmen of the Kalahari Desert, South Africa)

The Kalahari is one of the hardest places on earth for men to find food. The Bushmen hunt animals and collect wild fruits and vegetables. They do know that, outside their desert, other men live by raising animals and growing crops. Though they have not envied these men's way of life, the Bushmen do tell a story which explains how it happened that they became hunters and gatherers and not herdsmen and farmers like everybody else.

It was all the fault of the simple Kara-tuma. He was the first man in the world and the father of all Bushmen. The second man on earth was a cunning Bantu, the father of most of the other people who now live in southern Africa.

Looking for something to eat, Kara-tuma came across a cow. He seized it and was about to kill it when the Bantu came up.

This man said: "Don't harm it – I'll help you make it a kraal." So together they built a pen out of thorn trees and put the cow inside.

The Bantu now milked the cow. He gave Kara-tuma a small share of the milk.

Hanging on a tree was a strong strip of leather and a thin length of string. The Bantu at once seized the leather and made a halter for the cow.

He said: "This cow's mine now."

Kara-tuma had taken down the string. With it he made a snare and went off to hunt.

Soon after, Kara-tuma was digging a lizard out of its hole. This was in the middle of a patch of wild sorghum. The sorghum stalks were very scratchy and so, to get them out of the way, Kara-tuma set light to them.

Again the Bantu was passing. "You fool!" he cried. "You can eat this!" He tore up the few stalks the fire had not burnt and went away to plant the seeds.

The Bushmen say that, ever since those first days, Kara-tuma has left them no choice but to be hunters of animals and gatherers of wild plants.

How men first got fire

(Bushmen of the Kalahari Desert, South Africa)

One of the best toys which the boys make is called the *djani*. They take a strong reed. To one tip they tie a thread with a mangetti nut threaded on the end. On the other tip they glue a piece of guinea-fowl down. Each boy has a stick. They throw the *djani* up in the air . . . it floats slowly down, spinning as it falls, helped by a guinea-fowl feather stuck in the reed towards the upper, lighter tip . . . the nearest boy catches it on his stick and at once flings it up into the air again . . . everybody runs after it, to try and catch it when it falls again.

Once only Ka Kani had fire. With it he cooked food for himself and his children. One day a Bushman called Huwe went to visit Ka Kani. He was given a piece of roasted antelope meat to eat.

"Mmm . . . what a funny taste – it's delicious! What have you done to this meat?" asked Huwe.

A boy said: "We put it over the fire."

"So that it gets very hot," added his sister.

"Then it turns from red to brown," put in another boy.

"And that's what makes it taste so good," ended Ka Kani's smaller daughter.

But of course Huwe did not really understand them, as he had never seen fire. So the next day he crept back to Ka Kani's camp.

Ka Kani spent part of the day prodding up roots with his digging stick. Then Huwe saw him take some pieces of wood out of a hollow tree.

So he crept nearer. Ka Kani was twirling one stick in a hole in the other, saying all the time: "Fire will come, fire will come. . . ."

After a while, to Huwe's amazement, the sticks began to smoke. Ka Kani hastily dropped some scraps of dry bark into the smoking hole, then blew gently but steadily into it. Huwe saw a reddening. Ka Kani quickly and carefully tipped the bark into a ball of dry grass and, after he had blown on this too, a yellow flame crept out and upwards. Soon Ka Kani was cooking a potful of roots over a blazing fire.

The next day, Huwe walked into Ka Kani's camp again. They talked for a while and then Huwe said:

"How about playing *djani* with the children for a while – I've just made a new one." He showed Ka Kani and the boys and girls the toy he had brought with him.

One of the boys threw it into the air. "Look how well it flies!" he shouted.

They all ran after the *djani* as it drifted away in the wind. For Huwe had used some very special feathers and down, much lighter than those of even the guinea fowl, and so the new *djani* floated along on the air.

Little by little, the boys and girls and their father, Ka Kani, wandered away from their camp, following the *djani* as, going up and down, it drifted across the desert. Huwe muttered that he needed something from his bag, left at the camp. The game was so exciting that nobody noticed him go back.

Huwe ran to Ka Kani's camp and, taking the fire-sticks out of the hollow tree, broke them into a million pieces and threw them over the whole world. Since then there has been fire in all wood and men everywhere have been able to cook their food and keep warm on cold days.

The parrot that brought autumn

(Ona people, Tierra del Fuego)

The Ona people – who have vanished for ever – were hunters. They spent a lot of their time chasing animals in the forest. They used to say that, long long ago, before even their grandfathers and grandmothers were boys and girls, the forest had been green all the year round. The trees only lost their leaves when they died.

One day a boy called Kamshoat was making himself his first full-sized hunting bow. An old man came to speak to him.

"Kamshoat, it's time you went on the journey," he said.

The boy understood. He was now old enough to become a man. He would be told the secrets of his people and then would travel on his own to some distant land – this was to teach him to look after himself.

After a special ceremony for all the boys of about his age, Kamshoat began to get ready for his journey. He put on his warmest fur cloak and hat; it was a very cold land, with strong winds most of the year and often freezing rain and snow too. Taking only his new bow and a stone knife, Kamshoat walked away northwards.

Well, his adventures were too many to tell here. He saw great mountains with rivers of ice running down their sides and others with flames bursting from their tops. He hunted animals he had never seen before and made friends of people who lived in ways very different from those of the Ona.

Kamshoat was away for so long that his family and friends gave him up for dead. But one day, still in his old cloak and with his well-worn bow over his shoulder, Kamshoat walked back into his home camp.

The people gathered round him, looking at his hat – because it was made of a fur new to everybody – and asking him questions. Kamshoat had so much to tell them about that he forgot the rule that young men of his age were supposed to be silent and thoughtful.

"What were the forests like?" asked a friend.

"Huge," he answered. "Much bigger than ours, they just go on and on. And the strange thing is that every winter the trees lose all their leaves and seem to die, but in the summer they come to life again and the leaves come out as green as before!"

At this all the people laughed. A man said: "I wonder if we can believe *anything* Kamshoat has told us."

A boy said: "How can a tree come to life again, once it's dead?"

Kamshoat now started to tell the Ona about the strange animals he had seen, but by now people were walking off and even his family and friends were looking at him in a strange way. Kamshoat was very upset at this.

He spent a few days in the camp. Then, feeling unhappy and annoyed at the way he was still being laughed at, he suddenly left again.

But he was not away for long. For soon a huge parrot, with green feathers on its back and red and yellow ones on its chest, came flying through the forest. It was Kamshoat, although nobody guessed.

The parrot now flew all over the forest, painting each tree's leaves red and yellow with the colours on his chest. And then the leaves all fell to the ground!

Now it was the Ona people who were upset, for in the forest lived many of the animals which they hunted. If the trees died then the animals would go away and live somewhere else.

And now it was Kamshoat who laughed. The mocking cries of the great parrot rang through the forest. The Ona hunted him with their bows and arrows but of course Kamshoat – the parrot – knew their ways and always flew off in time.

But then, in the spring, the warm weather did bring the trees to life again. The people were delighted to see the buds and then the leaves spreading over the branches. Soon everybody was happy again.

The story isn't quite over, though. For the forest where the Ona used to live is now alive with the brightly-coloured parrots. They stay there even in the winter, though they look very much out of place up on the snow-covered branches. And they are very noisy: sitting together up in the trees, they make great fun of any men who happen to pass through the forest, mocking them for not having believed Kamshoat, their father of long ago.

The red-chested monkeys

(Ao Nagas of Assam, India)

Assam, where this story takes place, is a mountainous land covered with rich jungle holding many types of birds and animals. In a village lived a man with two sons. His wife had died and he had married again. But his happiness was mixed with sadness: his new wife did not like his two sons.

Early one morning he heard his oldest son say to the woman: "Please could we have some new clothes; it's cold working in the rice fields . . . you see, our clothes are worn out." The two boys really were almost naked.

The woman answered: "Next year, perhaps."

The younger boy then asked: "Please may we have some good food – we've eaten nothing but rice-husks for a long time." The two boys were both very thin.

The woman replied: "After the harvest . . . perhaps."

The two boys looked at each other sadly. They picked up their tools and, saying nothing more, walked slowly off to the rice-fields.

The father worked all day in the vegetable patch near the house. In the evening he was surprised to find that his sons had not come home.

So the next morning he decided to go and look for them. When his wife saw him putting food into a bag, she was cross. And when he rolled up two strips of red cloth for the boys to wear, she was even more annoyed. But there was nothing she could do, as the man had decided that he would now look after his sons.

When he reached the rice-fields, he saw the two boys among the trees on the further side. But they at once ran away. Surprised and saddened, the man put down his bundle in the middle of the field. Then, instead of going home, he hid behind a tree near the path.

After a while the two boys came back. Slowly, they went towards the bundle. Their father was amazed to hear that they did not speak to each other but instead chattered and shrieked, making sounds which he had never heard from them before. And then, as they came nearer to him, he saw they were covered in hair.

At this moment his sons picked up the red cloths and wrapped them round their chests. Then, with excited cries, they snatched up the food and fled with it to the trees – and were soon up in the branches.

The father wept, for he realized what had happened to his sons. They were in fact the first of the red-chested monkeys which now live in the Assam jungle.

Why a dog will always try to bite a goat

(Ao Nagas of Assam, India)

Two animals were getting married. Nobody can remember which ones – perhaps it was two elephants, or two tigers, or two wild buffaloes, for all these and many more live in the forests and mountains of Assam.

Anyway, among the guests at the feast were the Dog and the Goat. Now in those days the Dog had a fine pair of horns which he wore as people wear hats or crowns. During the feast, the Dog took off the horns.

The Goat came up and said politely: "Please can I try on your horns . . . just to see what they're like."

The Dog nodded. "It's very hot here, that's why I've taken them off," he replied.

The Goat fitted them on and then, liking the way he looked and thinking the horns would be useful, he ran off. And the dog never got his horns back. Ever since, dogs have attacked goats as soon as they see them – and the goats defend themselves with their stolen horns.

The right of mice to rice

(Angami Nagas of Assam, India)

"Look!" cried a man as he and some others were walking beside a lake. "There's a strange plant growing out there. I don't know why but something makes me think it would be good to eat."

While his friends waited, the man tried to wade out to the plant, but he found the water was too deep. He went back to the bank and stood there wondering how he could reach the plant. His friends walked on ahead.

A low voice said: "I'll go and get some of the seeds for you, if you like."

The man looked round and among the plants growing on the bank saw a mouse. "All right," he said.

So the mouse swam out and was soon back with a few seeds. It said to the man: "Here you are – it's a rice plant."

"Thank you," said the man. He went away and sowed the seeds in one of his fields which was flooded every time the great rains fell. He did this because he understood plants and could see that the rice liked to grow in a lot of water.

After several plantings and harvests, the man found he had enough rice to feed himself and his family for a long time. So he decided to reward the mouse.

He went back to the lake. The one rice-plant was still growing there. Looking around, he soon found the mouse in the bushes. The man told it how the rice had grown so well and then said: "I want you to have a share, as you brought in the seeds. If you'll come to my house, I'll give you a sackful."

The mouse replied: "Well, thank you very much. But my head is so small that I couldn't carry a sack of rice on it. Instead, could I come every day and eat a few grains?"

The man willingly agreed. Ever since, the mice have gone each day to men's rice-stores for their meals.

The old woman's animals

(Angami Nagas of Assam, India)

There was a time when all the animals were wild, looking after themselves in the forests, around the lakes and up in the mountains. The people hunted the animals if they wanted meat, furs and skins and, because the animals would not live with them, they had to do without milk and had to carry their loads on their backs.

The old woman who changed all this lived alone but for a daughter. One evening, on the way back from the rice-fields, the old woman felt a pair of hands over her eyes.

It was Zize, a spirit. "I'll let you go if you'll give me your daughter as a wife," he said.

The old woman promised and the next day the spirit carried off the girl as she walked some way behind her friends on their way back home from the rice-fields.

A year went by and then the girl came back to see her mother. After a few days, she said to the old woman: "Please come back with me now, to spend a little while at my new home."

So the mother and daughter set off to the spirit's house. The old woman took care to mark the way with a trail of rice husks.

When they were almost there, the girl said: "One important thing; as a gift when you leave, ask for the little basket which hangs in the centre room of our house, to the right as you go in."

The mother's stay passed quietly. But, when she was about to leave and asked for the basket, Zize tried very hard not to give it to her.

In the end, he said: "Very well, you can have it, but on three conditions. You mustn't open it on the way home and, when you get there, you must build a fence round the basket before you do open it, and then, for five days, you must take special care of what's inside it."

The old woman said goodbye to her daughter and to Zize. Following the trail of rice-husks, she walked along with the little basket under her arm.

"I wonder what's inside it . . ." she said to herself every few steps.

Her curiosity won. She put down the basket and undid the string fastening down its lid. As she was about to lift this she heard growlings, twitterings and squeakings coming from inside. She tried to do up the lid again but it was too late – it was flung back and out poured bears, birds, mice, monkeys . . . in an endless stream they ran and flew and scampered away into the forest!

"Oh, dear, look what I've done now!" cried the old

woman. Then with great determination, she threw herself on the basket and managed to close the lid, though she was not quick enough to stop a snake slipping out. "I think there are still a few animals left inside," she said to herself. "I heard a mooing and a grunting and a barking just before I closed the lid." She sat on the basket for a while, to get her breath back.

That night she reached home. The next morning she asked her friends to help her build a fence right around her house. Then she opened the basket . . . and out poured cows and buffaloes and pigs and chickens and several sorts of dogs, all mooing and snorting and squawking and barking at being out in the open again. They tried to run off too – since they were still wild animals – but the fence stopped them.

The old woman and her friends cut and collected up food for the animals, took them water and made them shelters. After five days, all the different animals had settled down in their new home.

A year later the old woman's daughter, this time with Zize the spirit, came on another visit. The little house and the ground around it were full of animals.

These are the animals which today live with man. The Nagas say that, if the old woman had not opened the basket while she was coming home, all the animals which are still wild would also be tamed too.

The fish and the wagtail

(Ainu people, Japan)

The Ainu say their god made the world. At first it was floating on the oceans but then it came to rest on the back of a great fish. The tides come and go as the fish sucks the sea in and out of its mouth. When the fish moves, the earth quakes.

Soon after he had created the world, the Ainu's god had to send two spirits to hold the fish down: ever since they have stood one on each side, a hand on its back. If children are seen eating with only one hand, they are told: "You mustn't do that, only the two spirits who have each to keep a hand on the great fish are allowed to eat like that!"

Having made the world, the Ainu's god still had to get it in order. So he brought a water wagtail down from heaven. The god then went about creating hills and valleys with his digging tool. The water wagtail, following him round, patted the land smooth with his tail . . . which he has wagged up and down ever since.

The hairy demon and the hunter

(Ainu people, Japan)

The land where the Ainu live has its share of the world's gnats, mosquitoes and biting flies – but,

worse still, long ago its mountains held a huge demon with a single eye as big as a potlid in the middle of its forehead. It was covered in hair rather like a bear, though it could not have been a bear since the Ainu treat this animal as sacred. The demon ate all those who went to hunt in the mountains.

All except one. Hearing about the demon, a young man took up his bow and arrows and climbed to where it lived. He shot an arrow straight at the great glaring eye. The much-feared demon was dead.

To make sure it could not come back to life, the hunter burned its body and spread the ashes across the land. And the ashes turned into gnats, mosquitoes and biting flies.

But the Ainu, a gentle and friendly people who usually accept the world as they find it, say it is wrong to grumble at such little troubles. After all, the hairy one-eyed demon was not satisfied with just a little bite – he ate everybody from top to toe!

The hedgehog and the fox

(Sahrawi nomads of West Sahara)

In the desert they say that even the longest road has a well at the end. All roads there seem especially long because there are no trees and no water, nothing but the hottest of suns and endless sand and rocks. Once upon a time, the Hedgehog and the Fox found themselves travelling together across this desert.

The Hedgehog was very tired. "Brother, shall we rest a while?" he asked his companion.

"Yes, let's," agreed the Fox. "We can get some shade over there."

Beside the track was the great skeleton of a dead camel.

They lay down to sleep. But, once the Fox was snoring, the Hedgehog crept away, taking with him some pieces of camel skin. Working quickly with his teeth and paws and a little knife he always carried with him, he made a rough saddle and a couple of reins. Then, running as fast as his short legs would go, he raced along the track until he reached a rock. On this he put the saddle. Then he ran back to their shelter and lay down. Soon he was asleep.

The sun moved round and the heat woke the Fox. "Eh, brother Hedgehog, perhaps we should be getting on."

The Hedgehog yawned and stretched and scratched. "It's a long road ahead," he replied.

They set off.

At once the Hedgehog said: "Do you know, I had a funny dream. I dreamt that, on the road, we'll find a saddle."

The Fox smiled.

The Hedgehog went on: "Suppose we do – let's agree that the one whom it fits will carry the other for the rest of the journey."

The Fox, who did not think that such a dream could ever be more than a dream, treated it as a joke and replied: "Yes, if you like."

Of course they soon found the saddle – and you can guess whom it fitted. In the Western Sahara the Hedgehog always gets the better of everybody else.

Counting the rows of barley

(Sahrawi nomads of West Sahara)

The people who live in the desert have to move about looking for food for their camels, sheep and goats. But, if they think it is going to rain, then they sow patches of good ground with barley and come back when it is ready to harvest.

One day the Hedgehog got talking to the Ostrich near a barley field. By now the grain was very tall.

The Ostrich said: "Life must be hard when you're only half as high as a barley stalk!"

The Hedgehog felt this was very rude. He looked thoughtfully up at the great bird. After a moment, he said: "I may be small but I make up for it by being able to run faster than anybody else in the desert."

"Ha! Ha!" cackled the Ostrich. "Why, I can run faster than the wind!" The tears rolled down its feathered cheeks.

"Want to bet?" asked the Hedgehog. "Suppose we see who's the quickest to count the number of rows of barley in this field?"

"All right," spluttered the Ostrich.

They agreed to meet at noon the next day. The Hedgehog and the Ostrich each spent the time going round to invite their friends to the race.

The sun was high above as the Hedgehog and the Ostrich met at one end of the field. The Ostrich smiled down at the Hedgehog. The Hedgehog was looking very serious. Over the top of the barley the

Ostrich waved a wing at his friends who were standing in a row at the other end of the field. The Ostrich supposed the Hedgehog's friends were there too – they would be too small to be seen over the barley stalks.

"Ready? Go!" cried the Hedgehog and the Ostrich together.

The Hedgehog disappeared into the barley but the Ostrich strode across the stalks. The smile was still on his face.

"One – two – three – four . . ." shouted the Ostrich as, with huge strides, he passed over the grain.

"Three – four – five – six . . ." cried the voice of the Hedgehog from deep in the barley.

The Ostrich's eyes opened wide in surprise. He began to run: "Five – six – seven – eight – nine!" he screamed.

"Eight – nine – ten – eleven – twelve . . ." came the calm counting of the Hedgehog, now three rows ahead.

The smile had by now left the face of the Ostrich. He almost flew over the stalks: "Ten – eleven – twelve – thirteen . . ." he croaked.

There were fifteen rows of barley in the field. With a final leap, the Ostrich hurtled over the last two lines.

"I've won!" he shrieked, crashing into his astonished friends.

But then he saw that the Hedgehog, sitting calmly on a rock and not at all out of breath, was there already. The Ostrich was so upset that it took his friends a long time to make him feel better about it.

The silly bird never thought to wonder where the Hedgehog's friends had been during the race . . . and of course, unless you're a hedgehog, it *is* difficult to tell one hedgehog from another.

Akaiyan and the beavers

(Blackfeet people of North America)

Long ago the Blackfeet made their tools out of stones and used dogs instead of horses to move their belongings from camp to camp. It was during this time that a young man called Akaiyan found himself left behind on an island in the middle of a great lake. He had gone there with his brother to get the feathers which fell from the many ducks and geese which nested there. The feathers were for making into arrow flights. But Akaiyan's brother had deliberately paddled away with their canoe while Akaiyan was at the other end of the island, because there was bad feeling between them.

Akaiyan sat down and wept, for the winter was coming on and he thought he would soon die from cold and lack of food. He now called on the animals to help him. Then he asked the spirits of the water to come to his aid. Finally he prayed to the sun, the moon and the stars. After he had done all these things he felt calmer and stronger.

So he began to make a shelter out of branches. And he gathered up all the feathers which were scattered around the island. He lay on them at night. They were so warm that, although it was getting colder and colder, he always slept well. During the daytime he hunted duck and geese, until they left to fly off to the south. By then Akaiyan had made himself a warm robe out of bird-skins, stitching them together with thread he made out of the bark of an alder tree. He had also hung up many dead birds as food for the winter. But although Akaiyan now felt he had a fair chance of living through the cold months ahead, he was sad at being away from his home and his friends.

One day he found himself in a part of the island where he had not been before. Here, in a small bay at the mouth of a stream, there was a beaver lodge (the Blackfeet call their own dwellings "lodges"). Akaiyan lay on the ground, watching. The sight of the family of beavers going in and out made him sad again. While he was weeping, he suddenly heard a voice.

"My father wants you to come into our lodge." It was a little beaver.

Akaiyan willingly went with him. Inside, under the roof of carefully-laid sticks, were seated a big beaver, his wife and the other children. The father was silver-haired from the many moons for which he had lived. Akaiyan thought he must be the head of all beavers. When he had told him his story, the great beaver said:

"Don't worry, you can stay here with us. We'll soon be closing up for the winter, just as soon as the water starts to freeze over. We do this every year – and we won't be going out again until the warm air in the spring melts the lake."

Akaiyan felt much happier when he heard this. "Thank you," he said, smiling for the first time since he had been left behind on the island.

"And we'll teach you everything we know – and we know a lot of wonderful things. Then you can tell them to your people when you get home."

Akaiyan brought his stores to the lodge. By then the beavers were closing up their dwelling, leaving only an air-hole in the top. Gradually it got colder and colder but the furry beavers kept Akaiyan warm

by laying their tails across him. They talked a lot.
Akaiyan made friends with them all, but especially
with the little beaver. Of all the children, the little
beaver was also the great beaver's favourite.

The beavers taught Akaiyan how to cure the sick
with certain roots and herbs, by wearing special
paints, by dancing and singing and praying. Akaiyan
liked the way the beavers beat time with their tails.
He listened to them very carefully – and all this later
became known as the Beaver Medicine Ceremony,
still used today by the Blackfeet people.

The beavers made a scratch on the wall of the lodge
every day. The passage of each moon they marked
with a stick. "There are seven moons between the
time the leaves fall and the day when, in the spring,
we open the lodge again. But listen! You can hear the
ice breaking – the day's getting near. . . ."

The little beaver now said quietly to Akaiyan:
"Before you leave, Father will give you anything you
like – choose me, I have the power to help you and
your people. Father will ask you four times to choose
something else, but you must always ask for me."

The next day the beavers did open the lodge again.
Overhead, flying north, were the ducks and geese –
some came down to live on the island. The great
beaver said: "Akaiyan, now that you'll be leaving us
. . . please choose anything from here to take with
you."

Akaiyan replied: "Thank you – I'd like little beaver
to come with me."

The great beaver looked sad at this, but after he had asked Akaiyan to choose four more times, he said: "Well, you're very wise. Little beaver is both the best worker and the one who knows most. I'm sorry to lose him but I will let him go with you. One last thing," he added. "Collect up a Medicine Bundle like the one you saw we use in our ceremony."

A canoe soon came in sight. It was paddled by some Blackfeet who had come to collect feathers for their arrows. They were very surprised to see Akaiyan. Because, although his brother knew what had happened to him, everybody had thought he was dead. They took him and the little beaver back to his camp.

The Blackfeet people were very pleased to be taught all that Akaiyan had learnt from the beavers. Helped by the little beaver, he had soon collected a Bundle.

The next spring Akaiyan asked all the animals to add their power to the Bundle. The elk and his wife gave a song and a dance, as did the moose and his wife. The woodpecker gave three songs and a dance. Of all the animals, only the frog could not dance or sing and so has nothing in the Bundle. The turtle could not either but he was lent a song by the lizard, who owned two songs.

Yet another winter passed and then, in the third spring of this story, Akaiyan took the little beaver back to his family on the island. And he went every spring to visit the lodge. The great silver-haired beaver always gave him a gift to add to the sacred Bundle. Akaiyan led the Beaver Medicine Ceremony amongst his people until he died. Both it and the Bundle have been handed down by the Blackfeet ever since.

The bad boy and the colours in the sun

(Thompson River people of North America)

"We'll leave him to look after himself for a few months," said his father.

"Yes, perhaps it'll do him good, he's such a bad boy," replied his mother.

Their son was lazy and made a lot of trouble and was always quarrelling with his friends. It was spring, the time when everybody left the underground lodges in which they had lived all winter and went up into the mountains. So, one day when the boy was away from home on a walk, his parents and the four other families who lived roundabout quickly packed up their things and set off to hunt deer in the high lands.

The boy came back and found the lodges empty. He tried to follow his family and the neighbours but a bird which makes a noise like a man whistling made him lose their tracks. So he came sadly back home again. "They left me behind deliberately," he thought to himself.

Just then the boy heard a creak from a big upside-down basket in a corner of the lodge. He turned it over and found his grandmother sitting underneath.

"They left me behind too, because I'm too old to go to the mountains any more," said the little woman. "Well, we can keep each other company. But you'll have to work to get us food."

So she showed the boy how to make himself a small bow and some arrows. With these he hunted mice for their food. The grandmother made the skins into a large blanket.

Then the boy taught himself to hunt the blue jays and then the magpies and then a bird whose name nobody now remembers. His grandmother made a blanket of the skins of each sort of bird.

One day the four blankets were spread out on the ground outside the lodge. Each was a different colour. The sun saw them as he was passing overhead. Though he wore robes at night, when he was at home, during the day he had always been naked.

"Boy!" roared the Sun. "Will you sell me those blankets?"

"Yes," said the boy, holding his hand over his eyes.

By the time his father and mother came back, the sun had taught the boy all sorts of useful skills in exchange for the blankets. The boy was no longer quarrelsome or lazy.

And since that day the sun has been wrapped in those robes – sometimes you can make out their colours.

How Rabbit caught the sun

(Omaha people of North America)

Rabbit lived with his grandmother. Early each morning, just after dawn, he would stick his head cautiously out of his hole, looking in all directions. His big ears would turn round and round as he listened. Then, if it was safe, he would go off hunting.

But, for as long as he could remember, somebody had always passed along his favourite trail before him. Rabbit could tell because this person always left a very long footprint. It made Rabbit cross – no matter how early he got up, there were the marks showing that somebody had already passed that way.

So Rabbit decided to set a trap. He made a noose out of an old bowstring and, one evening, fixed it across the path.

The next morning Rabbit got up early as usual. But when he put his head out of his burrow he found himself blinded by a dazzling light shining through the bushes and trees . . . shining from the path where he had set the trap.

Holding a paw to his eyes, Rabbit hopped slowly towards the light . . . from behind a tree-trunk, he

saw to his horror that he had caught the Sun in his
trap.

"How silly of me! Of course the Sun is the only
thing to be up before me – what am I going to do
now? It's so hot, I can't get near!"

Rabbit ran back to his hole. When his grandmother
heard what had happened, she said at once: "Look,
without the Sun the world will die. Today's going to
be a short day anyway now. You'll just have to go and
free the Sun."

So Rabbit took his knife and went up again.
Holding his breath, he ran into the great light and
luckily found his noose at once.

With a quick cut he freed the Sun. The light at once moved away through the trees and bushes. Rabbit's fur was badly scorched, especially between the shoulders while he was bending to cut the string. Because of this, all rabbits now have a brown spot between their shoulders, say the Omaha people.

The bears' tower

(Cheyenne people of North America)

Early one summer, three girls went out into the open
prairie to collect flowers for a festival. It had rained a
few days earlier and all the plants were now putting
out their most beautiful flowers.

The girls sang as they picked them. They tied them
into long strings and then wound them around their
necks.

Suddenly one gave a cry. The others looked round
to see three great brown bears running across the
prairie towards them.

"There's nobody to help us!" cried the first girl.

"We can't run as fast as the bears!" shouted the
second.

"There's nowhere to hide," said the third girl more
calmly, "but we can climb on to that rock over there."

So the three girls ran to the rock. Once on it, they
called out to the spirits for whose festival they had
been collecting the flowers. The bears were already
starting to climb up the sides of the rock. The first
was reaching out his huge clawed paw towards the
girls . . . when the little rock began to grow!

The hungry bears, growling and snarling, went on
climbing. But the rock went on growing.

Soon one bear was so tired – for the sides were
steep and slippery – that he let go, falling and being
killed on the ground far below. And then another
bear lost his grip and fell after him. Soon the third
bear also lay dead on the prairie at the foot of the
great rock.

The girls hugged each other in relief. Then one cried: "We'll never get down again!"

"Nobody will ever think to look for us up here!" cried the second.

"We'll make a rope out of the flowers," said the third girl.

So they plaited the strings of flowers into a thick rope. "It won't be long enough," cried the first girl.

"Or strong enough!" exclaimed the second.

"Let's pray to the spirits and then let the rope down," said the third girl.

They did so . . . and the rope stretched and stretched as they let it out. . . . It just reached the ground. The girls climbed down it and were soon home again.

The Cheyennes point out the great rock to travellers. It is certainly very strange the way it stands up all alone in the middle of the empty prairie – and the Cheyennes also say that you can see the scratches of the bears' claws down its sides.

The Old Man makes the world

(Blackfeet people of North America)

The Sun and the Moon were the father and mother of Napi, better known as the Old Man. They sent him on to the empty earth to create people and help them find a good way of life.

The Old Man travelled all over the earth, making mountains, prairies, forests, animals and birds. At last, coming from the south, the Old Man reached the land where the Blackfeet now live. This is the eastern side of the Rocky Mountains.

Once he had shaped the land there, the Old Man said to himself: "I could do with a rest."

So, clearing away some stones, he lay down on his back on a little hill. The Blackfeet know where this was, as the Old Man's shape can still be seen there.

Soon he set off again, but at once stumbled over a hillock, falling on his knees. The Old Man was rather cross. On the spot he raised a couple of rocks, still called The Knees today.

Next he made the Sweet Grass Hills. Then he covered the plains too with grasses. This way he made food for the animals he was about to form. He also marked off a piece of ground and sowed it with all kinds of eatable plants: carrots and turnips, serviceberries and bullberries, cherries and plums. Outside the patch he also planted all sorts of trees.

And then he created the animals. The Old Man stayed to see if they would be all right. The bighorn sheep – it has a huge head and horns to match – did not seem at home on the plains.

"Come on," said the Old Man, "you can try the mountains then." He took it up among the high dangerous rocks – and saw it happily leaping about amongst them. The Old Man decided to leave it up there.

But then he was very sorry to see an antelope run so fast across a mountain top that it fell over the edge. Luckily it was not badly hurt.

"You'd better come down onto the prairie," said the Old Man, lifting the animal off the mountainside. Once on flat open ground, the antelope ran gracefully away.

"Now . . ." said the Old Man thoughtfully, "next I'll make the first human beings."

He scooped up some soft clay and out of it shaped a man, a woman and a child. "You must become alive," he said to the three figures.

The Old Man then covered them up. Each morning he had a look to see how they were. Gradually they were turning into human beings.

On the fourth morning, the Old Man said to the figures: "Now stand up . . . and walk."

As they came to life, he said: "I'm called Napi."

He took the naked and helpless man, woman and child to the river to bathe. Next he showed them the roots and berries he had planted, saying: "These are good to eat." Then, pointing at certain trees, he added: "And you can also eat the bark of these – you just peel it away when it's young and soft."

The Old Man then decided to show the three new people where to find the herbs, leaves and roots which they would need to cure illnesses. So they went on a long journey across the prairies, the swamps and the forests.

"You do have to pick all these at the right times of the year," the Old Man explained.

By now the man, the woman and the child had seen the animals which the Old Man had made not long before. He said: "They're good to eat too." After a moment, he added: "And so are the birds."

So the Old Man cut a short strong shoot of a serviceberry plant. "You'll need weapons," he said. "First you peel off the bark . . . there – now you tie on a string and you've a bow."

The Old Man reached out and caught a passing bird. He pulled several feathers out of its wing, then let the squawking bird go again. He split a feather and fixed four pieces on the end of another smaller stick. "There, this is an arrow," he said, smoothing the feathers of the flight.

But when he fired the arrow it would not go straight. "Let's try it with only three pieces of feather. . . ." This time the arrow flew dead straight.

"Now you'll need good points for the arrows," muttered the Old Man, looking around. He tried all sorts of stones, breaking them up into sharp pointed pieces. "Black flint seems best," he said after a while. "And some of the white isn't bad either."

Then the Old Man taught the three human beings how to hunt with the bow and arrows.

"You can't eat meat raw, it'll be bad for you," he told them next. Picking up some dry scraps of rotten wood, the Old Man shredded it into soft pieces. Then he found a lump of very hard wood and, using one of the stone-tipped arrows, drilled a hole in it.

"You take this," he said to the man, giving him a stick of hard wood, "and put it in the hole and then twirl it between your hands. . . ."

The man did so and soon smoke came from the hole.

The Old Man said to the woman: "Quick, you drop in some pieces of the bark."

The woman did so and, within moments, they had caught fire.

"There you are," said the Old Man, smiling.

He watched the three humans as they tried to cook their meat. They were not sure how to do it.

"You need some dishes," the Old Man said. "Look!" He searched about and found a flat slab of soft rock and then a pointed lump of hard rock. "It takes a while," he said, starting to hollow out the first piece with the second piece. "Patience, that's another thing that you'll need." He passed the pieces of stone to them.

The Old Man now decided that he would move on the next day. So in the evening after the man, the woman and the child had enjoyed their first supper, he told them how a person could call for help from the spirits.

"You must first go away and sleep on your own somewhere. Then, in a dream, there will come a messenger to you, perhaps an animal: do as it says. In the same way, if you are travelling alone and need help, cry out aloud to the spirits and, through perhaps an eagle or a buffalo or a bear, help will come."

The Old Man then set off northwards. Many animals went with him, as servants – there was an understanding between them and the Old Man. Once he was beyond the Porcupine Hills he made some more people. This time he used mud and blew on them until they came to life. Then in the same way he made great herds of buffalo and sent them running across the plains.

"Those are especially for you, for your food," he said to the new people.

"But how do we kill them?" asked a man.

Old Man thought for a moment and then said: "You see that slope with a steep cliff on the other side – well, heap up some rocks at the bottom of the slope and hide behind them. . . ."

They did as the Old Man said. Then he drove the buffaloes towards them. As the animals neared the bottom of the slope, the Old Man bellowed: "Now jump out and frighten them so that they go up there!"

The buffaloes all galloped up the rising ground and, afraid of the people now chasing them, jumped over the cliff.

"There you are," pointed the Old Man. "The animals are dead at the foot of the cliff; they're there for you to eat."

The Old Man was about to move on again when a man came up to him and asked: "How do we get the skins off?"

Breaking some sharp pieces of stone off the cliff edge, the Old Man said: "Here are some knives." He went on: "You can put the skins on poles to make yourselves shelters against the cold and the rain." These are the round tents the Blackfeet have used ever since.

The Old Man went on northwards, creating the Bow and the Elbow Rivers. At their joining place he made and taught more people, again giving them herds of buffalo. By now he was so tired that he lay down on a hill near Red Deer River . . . here too you can still see his shape on the ground. Finally he reached a high mountain and, looking down over all he created in the region, was very pleased.

One side of the mountain was very slippery. The Old Man slid down it on to the plain. The Blackfeet now call the place "The Old Man's Sliding Ground".

Then he went away to the west. To the Blackfeet who saw him as he was leaving, he said: "I'll always be taking care of you wherever I am – and one day I *will* come back."

In the last hundred years, life has changed very much for the Blackfeet. The buffalo have all been killed by the white men from Europe – and some

Blackfeet think that when the Old Man does return he will bring with him more great herds of buffalo. But other Blackfeet say that the Old Man's last words were that, when he does come back, both the Blackfeet and the world will be very much changed.